This book belongs to:

Joanna ♡

I LOVE YOU

Printed in the U.S.A.

ISBN 0-7172-8278-3
Previously published as 0-681-40840-5

Jim Henson's
Muppet Babies
On the Go

by Emily Paul   illustrated by Kathy Spahr

GROLIER

Muppet Babies, how will you get where you're going?

Will you ride there on a bicycle
that's built for one or two?
Or a tricycle that has three wheels?
Now, that's the bike for you!

Will you roll there on some roller skates,
or learn to dip and glide
On a custom-crafted skateboard?
That's a thrilling way to ride!

Will you travel in a taxi or a buggy or a car?
Will you have to go a little way or is it very far?

Will you travel by a jeep
or in a shiny limousine
That your driver scrubs and polishes
so that it's squeaky clean?

Will you travel on a boat train
or a monorail up high?
Will you be aboard a freight train
or a railroad chugging by?

Will you travel on a subway,
    tunneled deep into the ground
Or by trolley? Why not trolley,
    if a trolley can be found?

Will you slip there on a steamer
or a sailboat flying free?
Will you float above the rolling waves
or swim beneath the sea?

Will it be an ocean liner or a submarine for you?
Or a rowboat or a tugboat or a pretty red canoe?

You can travel on a semi
(that's a tractor-trailer truck).
You can hop atop some big wheels
if you have a little luck.

You can move in an earth mover
    or upon a dump truck seat
Or travel in a tow truck
    down the middle of the street!

You can fly there in a plane
    or jet that soars up in the sky
Or take a rocket to the moon—
    now, that's the way to fly!

You can travel in a stately blimp,
   or take all afternoon...